Eddie, Tom and Mum were thinking about a holiday.

"This place looks nice," said Eddie.

"Mmmm," said Tom.

"We could go camping," said Mum.

"Yes! Yes!" shouted Lily and Tilly,

from their secret den.

They began to pack for the camping holiday.
Eddie packed his torch and recorder and toothbrush
and pyjamas in his rucksack. In his pockets he put
a notebook and pens, a compass, a whistle,
some pieces of string, and his Little Book of Knots.

Lily and Tilly packed too much.
"Start again," said Mum.

At last Tom began to load the car.

"What about Pusskin?"
asked Eddie.

"He can stay with Angie down
the road," said Tom. "Cats don't
like camping."

It was a long way to the campsite.

"When are we there?" said Lily.
"Are we there yet?" said Tilly.
"I'm not sure," said Tom.

They stopped for a picnic supper.
"Not far now," said Mum. "I think."

It was getting dark.
"Here we are," said Tom.

Eddie helped Tom
put up the tent.

"Hot chocolate for everybody?" said Mum.
But Lily and Tilly were nearly asleep already.

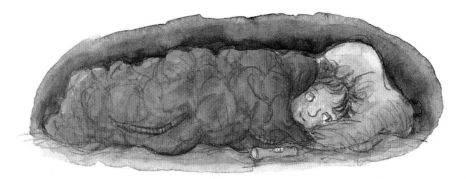

Eddie listened to the owls hooting, and to
the little creatures scuffling in the grass outside.
He pretended he was a boy living in the stone age,
a bold and fearless boy, safe in his cave.

Eddie woke up, and looked out of the tent
at the sun, rising over the sea.
  Mum, Lily, Tom and Tilly were still fast asleep.
  Eddie got dressed very quietly.

He walked down to the beach, through the dry, scratchy grass,
over hard stones and onto the soft sand.
The little waves made a peaceful, lapping noise.

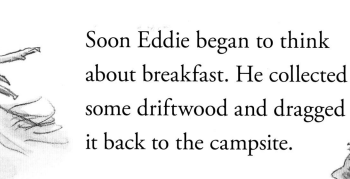

Soon Eddie began to think about breakfast. He collected some driftwood and dragged it back to the campsite.

"Firewood! Just what we need," said Tom.

He showed Eddie how to make a fire. They blew gently on the tiny flame to make it grow.

As the flame became stronger they put bigger twigs, then branches, on the fire.

Eddie helped Tom set up a pothook to heat water in the billy, and Tom began to fry the bacon.

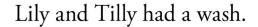

Lily and Tilly had a wash.

Mum mixed up flour and water
to make Damper Bread.
She wound the soft dough round
a stick, and held it over the fire.

When it was crisp and golden, they ate it with butter.
Even the burnt bits tasted good.
"Like smoke," said Lily.

"Let's get everything shipshape," said Mum.

She fetched stones to put round the campfire to make it safe. Tom put up a washing line, and Lily and Tilly helped him. Eddie used Tom's camping saw to make a useful mug-holder and plate-rack.

When the others went off to build sandcastles,
Eddie decided to make a tent of his own.
He looked behind some bushes and found
the perfect place.

He got some long sticks and bound them
tightly together with the string from his
pocket. Then he looked up which knots
to use from his little book.

He tied an old tarpaulin over the top for a roof.

Then he sat inside his tent and looked out at the sea.
He pretended he was wrecked on a desert island,
dreaming of fish and chips.

"Lunchtime!" called Mum.

Eddie ran back to the campsite. "Can we have fish and chips?" he said.

Everyone agreed that this was a good idea, so they set off for the fish-and-chip van.

They left the camp and went past a bench, along a path, over a gate, under an old dead tree and round a big dark wood.

On the way, Eddie stopped to draw a map of the journey in his notebook. He checked his compass so they wouldn't get lost on the way back.

By the time they reached the fish-and-chip van they were all very hungry, but Lily and Tilly began to fuss.

"*Eugh!* No fish for me," said Lily.
"Fish is *yuck!*" said Tilly.
"Just chips for you then," said Mum.

Eddie sat down to eat his fish and chips near a boy
with a puppy, who was fishing with his grandad.

"Have a go, if you like,"
said the boy.
"Thanks," said Eddie.
"Have some chips."
Soon they were friends.

The boy's name was Max, and his puppy
was called Bouncer. While Max looked at Eddie's
Little Book of Knots, Eddie had a go at fishing.

It wasn't long before something jerked hard on his fishing line.

"Wow!" shouted Eddie. "Help!" he cried, as something thrashed wildly about. "Hold tight," said Max's grandad. "You've caught a whopper!"

He helped Eddie reel in the fish, and scooped it up in his net. The fish was huge! Lily and Tilly screamed with excitement!

"Good work!" said Max's grandad. "Take it back for your supper. We've caught plenty of fish already." "Thanks very much," said Eddie.

Mum, Tom, Eddie, Lily and Tilly went back to the campsite a different way, along the beach. Sometimes they played tag, and sometimes they did handstands and cartwheels.

But then Eddie heard a shout. They all turned and saw Max racing towards them, with his grandad close behind him.

"Have you seen Bouncer?" panted Max. "I've lost him!" Eddie saw that Max was nearly crying.

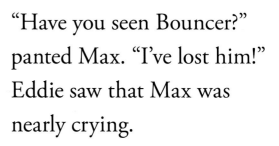

They all began to hunt for Bouncer.

Eddie and Max ran on ahead, but they ran too far.

Suddenly they found that they were lost too.

They were all alone in a big dark wood.

For a moment they were scared.

Then Eddie remembered his compass
and his map.
  "Don't worry, Max," he said.
They both looked at the compass,
and then at the map in Eddie's
notebook.

"Here's the old dead tree!"
said Eddie.
So they ran under it.

"There's the gate!" shouted Max.
So they climbed over it.

"This is the path!" panted Eddie.
So they ran down it.

"Onto the bench!" they cried together.
They stood on the bench and looked around.
There was the beach, so they weren't lost any more,
but still there was no Bouncer to be seen.

Now Eddie remembered his whistle.
He blew it loud and long. There was a reply!
They could hear it on the wind!
   "Yap yap!"
The boys ran towards the sound.

Eddie kept whistling,
and the yaps kept yapping,
and the yaps were coming
from Eddie's tent!

There, inside the tent,
was Bouncer, shivering
and scared, sheltering
from the wind.

And when Bouncer
saw Max he jumped
straight into his arms.

Eddie took a piece of string
from his pocket and tied it
to Bouncer's collar with
a reef knot.

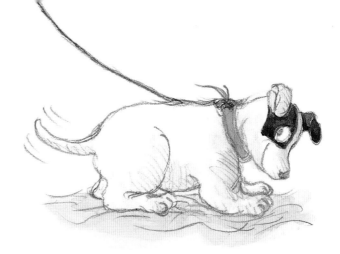

Just then, a search party arrived.
 "Eddie!" shouted Lily.
 "Bouncer!" shouted Tilly.
 Hey, Max!" shouted Max's grandad.
 "Great tent, Eddie!" said Tom and Mum.

They were all very glad to be together again.
"Let's have a celebration supper," said Mum.
"There's enough fish for everybody!"

Eddie and Max scrubbed potatoes
to be cooked in the ashes.

They sharpened twigs, to skewer
sausages and onions for roasting.

Tom prepared his special
baked chocolate bananas,
for pudding.

Max's grandad
prepared the big fish,

and Mum grilled it over the fire.

Lily and Tilly decided to make
a secret tent of their own.
It was rather small.

The fire crackled and blazed.

Sparks flew up like stars, into the starry sky.

Lily and Tilly thought they might try a very small piece of fish.

Then they had some more. And then they had even more.

Bouncer had several sausages.
Max's grandad had two whole chocolate bananas.
It was a feast!

After supper, Tom played his guitar and Eddie
played his recorder and Max banged a drum
made from a tin, and they all sang songs.

After that, Eddie and Max lay in the grass, looking at the moon.

"Let's meet up at your tent tomorrow," said Max.

"Great," said Eddie.

Suddenly Lily and Tilly were wide awake.

"Me too!" said Tilly.

"And me!" said Lily.

Some Tips for Camping

Sleeping out for even one night, in a tent in a field, is an adventure – especially for children. Being close to the earth and the elements, and learning practical and survival skills, gives confidence and an awareness of the world.

It is good to involve children with day-to-day jobs – clearing the camp site, fetching wood and water, and preparing and cooking food. If you can, practise putting up the tent in the garden before you leave, so you all know what you are doing when you get to the camping site.

Campfires

There are very good camping gas stoves on the market, but a real fire feels like the heart of a camp.

Make one in a permitted area, and don't light it on a very windy day. Build it in an open space, away from bushes, trees and scrub, and clear away any dry grass and weeds.

Put a ring of stones around the fire place to contain it.

Make a little heap of tinder in the fire ring. Tinder can be dry leaves, dry grass, small twigs, wood shavings or crumpled newspaper. Light the tinder. Or bypass all this and use a fire lighter.

Have ready some dry kindling – small sticks – and make an open structure around and over the tinder or fire lighter. This can be in a criss-cross or teepee shape, to let in plenty of air.

When the fire is burning well, add larger pieces of wood.

Don't leave the fire unattended.

Put it out completely whenever you leave it. Pour water over the ash, scatter it and cover with earth.

Camp Cooking

Plan meals and prepare the food together – living out of doors will make everyone hungry.

If you are cooking over a campfire, wait until the flames have died down and you are left with a bed of glowing embers. This intense, steady heat is best for cooking.

Aluminium foil is very useful. Potatoes can be baked directly in the ashes, but they often burn on the outside before they are cooked within. It is worth wrapping each one in aluminium foil first. Or, to make individual vegetable parcels, put a group of any vegetables you like on a piece of foil – a potato, a carrot, a sweet potato, an onion, maybe some garlic – sprinkle them with olive oil and salt and pepper, fold the foil into a parcel, seal the edges, and bury in the ashes. When they are tender, unwrap and eat with butter.

Here are two simple recipes from Eddie's camp.

Damper Bread

Damper Bread is delicious eaten warm. It is crusty on the outside, with a soft crumb, and it takes only a few minutes to prepare. The most basic recipe uses a handful of self-raising flour, a pinch of salt, and enough water to make a soft dough.

This richer, more delicious recipe uses some fat.
• Rub 28g/1oz butter into 225g/8oz self-raising flour and a pinch of salt.
• Stir in about 115ml/4fl.oz of milk. Spice up with cumin or poppy seeds or fresh herbs, if you like.
• Knead briefly, to bring the dough together, then squeeze and roll it between your hands until you have several long sausages, about 25mm/1inch in diameter.
• Wind these in spirals around long clean sticks, which are at least 25mm/1inch thick, squeezing a little as you go to hold them fast.
• Hold or prop them above the embers, turning every few minutes, until they are golden brown and cooked through. This could take fifteen minutes. (If you hurry they will burn on the outside and stay raw inside.)
• Slide them off the sticks. Eat hot, with butter, or wrapped with bacon, or stuffed with cheese.
This mixture also works well as a flatbread. Press balls of the dough into thin flat discs, and grill, or fry in a dry pan, until cooked through.

Chocolate Bananas

These are wonderfully easy to make.
• Simply cut a slit along the side of a whole banana, and slide in slivers of chocolate.
• Leave on a grill over the embers until the skin is black, the banana soft, and the chocolate melted.

Cooking Equipment

An iron grill or rack can be propped over the hot embers of a campfire, for grilling, barbecuing, and as a support for a wok, pan or billy.
A wok is a very good, multi-purpose piece of equipment. It is light, and easy to pack, and can be used for boiling, frying, stir frying and stewing. It is also good for heating water for washing and washing-up. Bring something to use as a lid, and a wire scoop.
An alternative is a deep frying pan – ideally in cast iron – with a lid or cover. This can be used for frying, and for simmering pasta or rice sauces.
A billy is useful for boiling water and vegetables, and for cooking pasta. Bring a chopping board, a wooden spoon and spatula, a tin opener, an oven glove and a sharp knife.

Basic food supplies might include: bottled water, long-life milk, flour, sugar, rice, salt and pepper, porridge oats, hot chocolate powder, biscuits, fruit including lemons, potatoes, onions and other vegetables, bacon and eggs, baked beans, tinned tomatoes, sunflower or olive oil, coffee and tea, and marshmallows for toasting.

First Aid

A first-aid box could include: insect repellant, spray for insect bites and burns, antihistamine cream, sun screen, paracetamol, a crepe bandage and safety pins, assorted plasters, scissors, antiseptic cream and antiseptic wipes.

Eddie's Camping Checklist

Eddie packs a torch so he can feel safe at night, a whistle to communicate with, a recorder for music, paper and pens to write and draw, and to draw maps, and a compass to help him find his way back to the camp.
And then there is his Little Book of Knots, and the string which always comes in handy.

Here are some suggestions for things to bring:

Water carrier, cool box, large plastic bowl, rope, clothes pegs, washing-up liquid, tea towel, dishcloth, tarpaulin, picnic rug, lantern, candles, matches or lighter, firelighters, rubbish bags, thermos, aluminium foil, kitchen roll, small saw, dry kindling and firewood, mugs, plates and cutlery.
Sleeping bags, pillows and towels, flannels, soap, toothpaste and toothbrushes, toilet paper and trowel.
Games, toys, books, paper and pens, musical instruments.
Torches and whistles, compass, umbrella, binoculars.
Sun hats, warm hats, wellies, swimwear, warm and waterproof clothes – prepare for all weathers!

A note on knots

As knots are of special interest to Eddie, here are two simple knots to start with:

The first is a **reef knot**, for fastening two ends of rope or string securely together, so they won't slip.

The second is a **clove hitch**, for tying a rope or string to a pole or tree.
Or for tying Bouncer's lead to a fence post.